To my delightful grandchildren, Isaiah and Wesley, and to those yet to come. You're the best!
Love, Gramma Sandy

AuthorHouse™
1663 Liberty Drive
Bloomington, IN 47403
www.authorhouse.com
Phone: 1-800-839-8640

First published by AuthorHouse 01/09/2012

ISBN: 978-1-4670-4267-3 (sc)

Library of Congress Control Number: 2011917427

Printed in the United States of America

This book is printed on acid-free paper.

authorHOUSE®

SLEEP COMES TO YOU

Sandy Fisher-Houghton

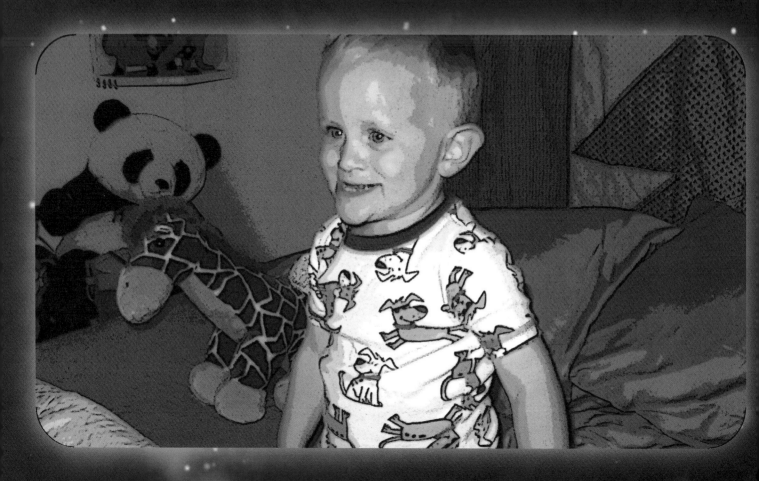

"I can't go to sleep Mom", the little one said.

Oh the tears and frustration, the gloom and the dread.

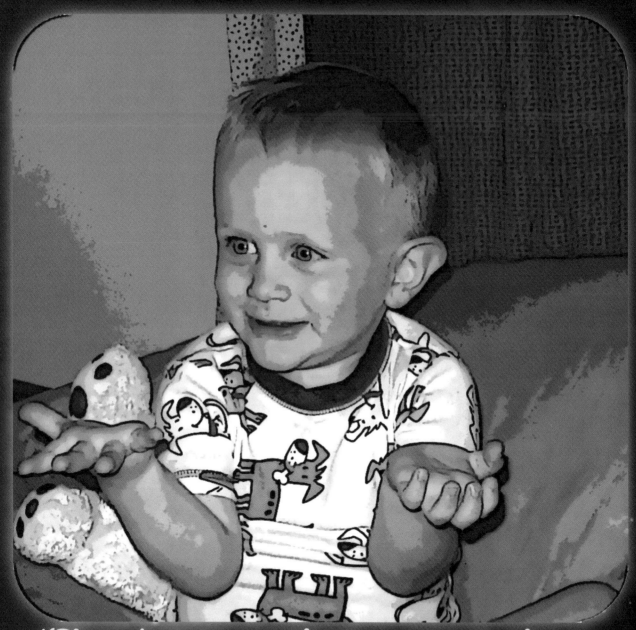

"I've been trying a long time, now what'll I do?"

"You don't go to sleep.
Sleep comes to you."

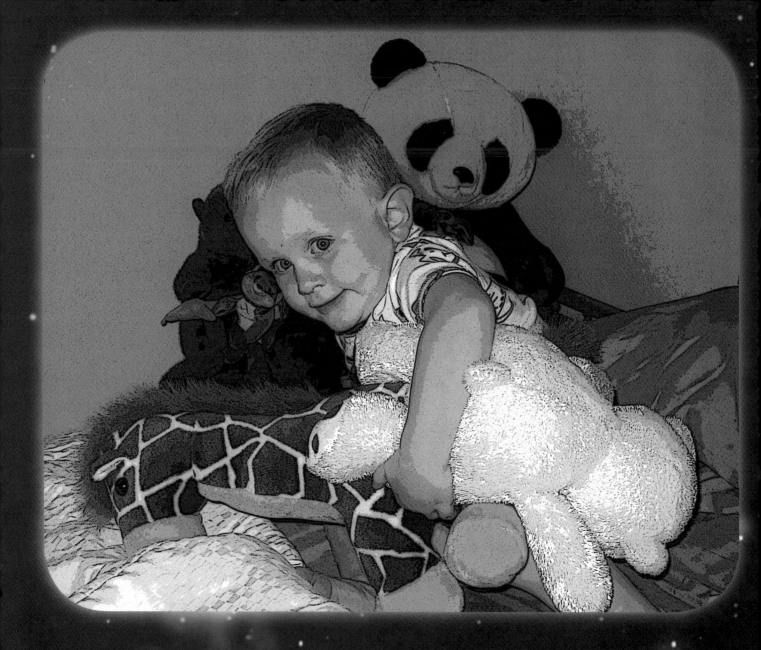

Still flipping and flopping,
Creating a sight,

More steaming

and scheming to stay up all night.

"One more sip of water?

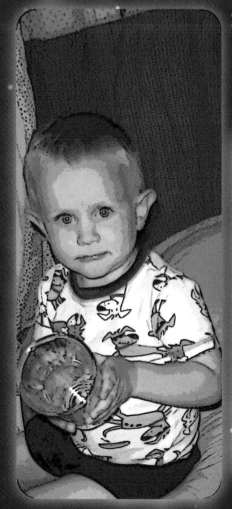
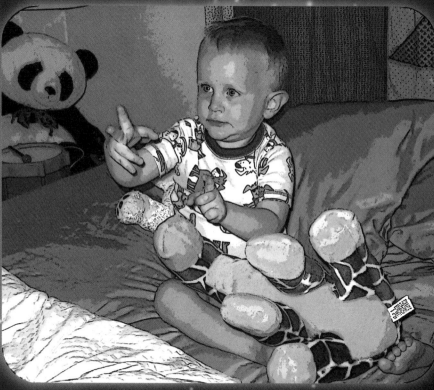

Another book? How 'bout two."

"You can't go to sleep dear?
Just let sleep come to you."

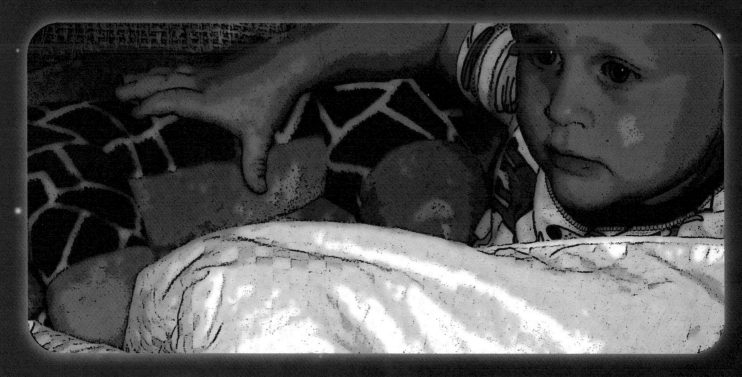

"It's too dark in here.
I need more light.
Don't close the door. I'm scared.
There's a noise outside!"

"I'm closing the window.
Better?
That's just the wind sweetheart.
And when sleep comes to you,
you won't see the dark."

"My nose is too stuffy and my ears won't pop."

"Excuses, excuses!
It's time now to stop.
Just take some deep breaths
and blow them out sloooowww.
Sleep will come before you know."

"I've done all you said and I can't go to sleep!"
"Have you counted your blessings instead of some sheep?"

"Then you'll need to lie still
as all children must do.
It's not wise to be bouncing
when sleep comes to you."

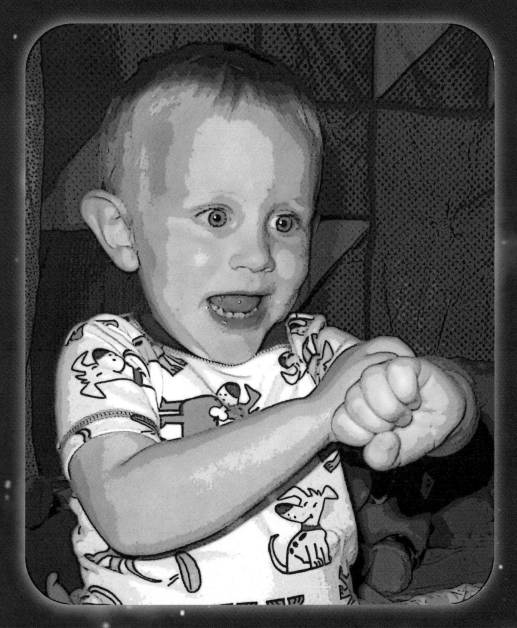

"Can we play a game Mom? I've got a bad itch."

"Ask the good-dream maker to flip your switch.

Then consider whatever is noble and true.
Don't try going to sleep.
Just let sleep come to you."

"Can we go to Grandma's house
on ... Sunday?

May I paint ...

and build
blocks ...

and run outside and
... play?

I'll still be awake in the morning
... you'll see

before sleep yyaaahhh...

ever hhomm.......aaahhh

comes...

to...

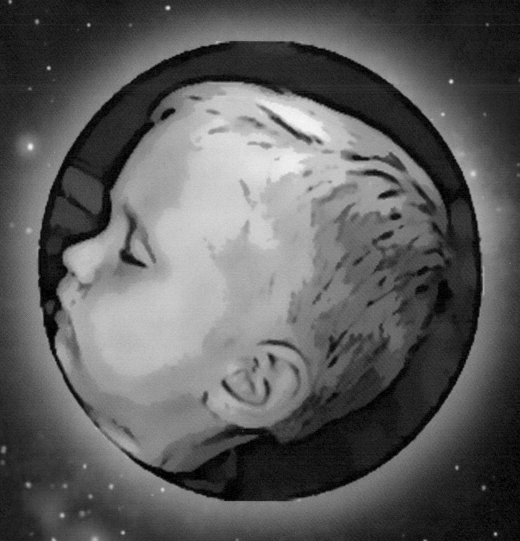

meeeeeee... zzzzzzzzzzz...

CPSIA information can be obtained
at www.ICGtesting.com
Printed in the USA
267735LV00001B